Dear Parent:

Your child's love of reading starts here!

Every child learns to read in a different way and at his or her own speed. Some go back and forth between reading levels and read favorite books again and again. Others read through each level in order. You can help your young reader improve and become more confident by encouraging his or her own interests and abilities. From books your child reads with you to the first books he or she reads alone, there are I Can Read Books for every stage of reading:

SHARED READING
Basic language, word repetition, and whimsical illustrations, ideal for sharing with your emergent reader

BEGINNING READING
Short sentences, familiar words, and simple concepts for children eager to read on their own

READING WITH HELP
Engaging stories, longer sentences, and language play for developing readers

READING ALONE
Complex plots, challenging vocabulary, and high-interest topics for the independent reader

I Can Read Books have introduced children to the joy of reading since 1957. Featuring award-winning authors and illustrators and a fabulous cast of beloved characters, I Can Read Books set the standard for beginning readers.

A lifetime of discovery begins with the magical words "I Can Read!"

Visit www.icanread.com for information on enriching your child's reading experience.

Clarion Books is an imprint of HarperCollins Publishers.
I Can Read® and I Can Read Book® are trademarks of HarperCollins Publishers.
Pretzel and the Puppies: Construction Pups
Copyright © 2022 by HarperCollins Publishers LLC
All rights reserved. Printed in the United States of America. No part of this book may be used
or reproduced in any manner whatsoever without written permission except in the case of brief
quotations embodied in critical articles and reviews. For information address HarperCollins Children's
Books, a division of HarperCollins Publishers, 195 Broadway, New York, NY 10007.
www.icanread.com

ISBN 978-0-35-868362-9 — ISBN 978-0-35-868363-6 (pbk.)

Typography by Stephanie Hays
22 23 24 25 26 LB 10 9 8 7 6 5 4 3 2 1
First Edition

I Can Read!
BEGINNING 1 READING

PRETZEL AND THE PUPPIES

CONSTRUCTION PUPS

Margret and H. A. Rey

CLARION BOOKS
An Imprint of HarperCollins*Publishers*

The construction dogs are hard at work.

They're building something new.

What could it be?

A store? A house?

Pedro, Puck, Paxton, Pippa, Poppy,

Pretzel, and Greta

cannot wait to find out!

"We've been working our tails off,"
Foredog Frida tells the pups.
"We built something for the city.
It's called the Bow Wow Tower."

The tower is tall.

The tower is round.

And from the top

you can see all of Muttgomery!

But if you use the binoculars,
you can see even better!

The pups can

see their house,

the lake,

the Bowl

restaurant,

and Kibble

Market.

They can even

see Nana!

"Hi Nana!" Pippa waves.

"She looks close,

but Nana is too far away to hear you,"

Pretzel reminds her.

The binoculars are amazing.

But some dogs can't reach.

They can't look in the binoculars.

They can't see all of Muttgomery.

"We wish we could see

what everyone else sees,"

they tell Poppy.

The pups think the binoculars

should work for every dog.

Can they fix them?

Time to get their paws up!

The binoculars move up and down.

When they tilt them down

the small dogs can reach.

But all they see is the sky.

If only they were taller!

They are taller when they
stand on Puck's back.
But he can't hold them up
long enough to be a good step stool.

That's it!

What little dogs need are step stools.

But where will they get those?

Could the pups make them?

The pups need some help.

They ask Foredog Frida.

The construction dogs

will build the step stools,

with a little help from the pups.

With their new hard hats

the pups are safe to work.

What supplies do they need?

Paxton and Pretzel

get some wood.

Foredog Frida and Poppy

mark where they'll cut the pieces.

The pups stand back.

Foredog Frida uses a saw.

The steps are shaped like bones!

Puck, Pedro, and Poppy

help Pretzel carry the pieces.

Then Pretzel brings them

to the top of the tower.

Foredog Frida uses a drill

to make holes for the screws.

Puck likes the sound it makes.

Poppy helps use a screwdriver

to put the pieces together.

The last thing to do

is to paint the stools.

Paxton uses bright colors.

When the step stools are done,

the pups show them to their friends.

"Welcome to the new and improved

Bow Wow Tower!" they say.

The small dogs try a step stool.

They can reach the binoculars!

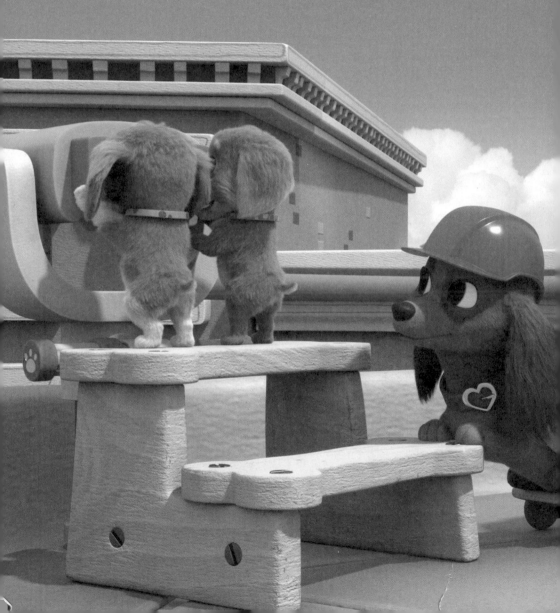

Now every dog
can enjoy the Bow Wow Tower.
Thanks, construction dogs!

Good job, construction pups.

You made a difference today.

You made your bark!